Kojo

Loves

Science

DR. ARTIKA TYNER

Planting People Growing Justice Press
P.O. Box 131894
Saint Paul, MN 55113
www.ppgjbooks.com

Printed and bound in the United States of America

First Edition
LCCN: 2022944534
LB ISBN: 978-1-9592232-0-7

Dedication

This book is dedicated to scholars of
Maxfield Elementary School.

Kojo's father always told him to dream big.

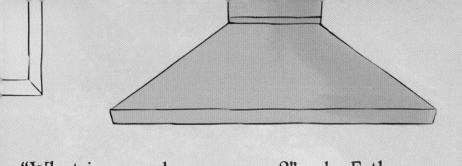

"What is your dream career?" asks Father.
"I want to be a scientist just like you, Daddy,"
Kojo says.

Kojo's father taught him about science every day. Kojo was excited to learn about STEM.

On Monday, they went to his father's lab. Kojo wore his father's lab coat as he watched his father experiment.

On Tuesday, they watched the rainfall. Kojo's father taught him about climates and seasons.

On Wednesday, they worked on coding. Kojo created his very first video game.

On Thursday, they built a model airplane.
Kojo dreamed of flying around the world.

On Friday, they visited an art gallery.
Kojo learned how to paint a map of Africa.

On Saturday, they volunteered at the local community garden. Kojo planted big red juicy tomatoes and sweet green peas.

On Sunday, they baked a sweet potato pie together. Kojo helped to read the recipe and measure the ingredients.

Kojo could not wait
to learn something
new each day
starting next week.

PARENTS AND EDUCATORS

Children are naturally curious and creative. They like to play, tinker, build, and explore. These are all key components of STEM education. Imagine creating learning opportunities to help introduce children to STEM learning early. This would aid children in developing core competencies like communication, confidence, critical thinking, and collaboration.

STEM education will also prepare children for the future. STEM careers are booming. STEM careers are among the top fastest-growing careers, growing two times faster than all other careers combined (Bureau of Labor Statistics).

How can you support your child/ren as they learn more about STEM?

- Talk about STEM: Share about careers in STEM to support early career exploration.

- Make an impact: Show your child how STEM can make a difference in the world, from addressing climate change to protecting endangered species.

- Unleash creativity: Encourage your child to become a lead problem solver.

- Build together in a team: STEM is about teamwork. Provide opportunities for your child to learn together with other children.

- Do STEM activities at home: Make STEM a part of daily learning, from learning math while budgeting to cooking in the kitchen while learning the basics of chemistry.

- Find ways to make learning interactive and fun.

Don't forget the "A" in STEAM. The "A" represents the arts. This is an integral part of learning about STEM by fostering creativity and innovation.

ABOUT THE AUTHOR

Dr. Artika R. Tyner is a passionate educator, an award-winning author, a civil rights attorney, a sought-after speaker, and an advocate for justice committed to helping children discover their leadership potential and serve as change agents in the global community. She is the founder/CEO of Planting People Growing Justice LLC.

PLANTING PEOPLE
GROWING JUSTICE

About Planting People Growing Justice Leadership Institute

Planting People Growing Justice Leadership Institute seeks to plant seeds of social change through education, training, and community outreach.

A portion of proceeds from this book will support the educational programming of Planting People Growing Justice Leadership Institute.

Learn more at www.ppgjli.org